BIG BEAR HUG

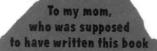

**To my mom,
who was supposed
to have written this book**

Text and illustrations © 2009 Nicholas Oldland

This edition is only available for distribution through the school market by
Scholastic Book Fairs and Scholastic Canada, Ltd

ISBN 978-1-55453-482-1 (pbk.)

CM PA 09 0 9 8 7 6 5 4 3 2 1

Kids Can Press acknowledges the financial support of the Government of Ontario,
through the Ontario Media Development Corporation's Ontario Book
Initiative; the Ontario Arts Council; the Canada Council for the Arts;
and the Government of Canada, through the BPIDP, for our publishing activity.

Published in Canada by
Kids Can Press Ltd.
29 Birch Avenue
Toronto, ON M4V 1E2

Published in the U.S. by
Kids Can Press Ltd.
2250 Military Road
Tonawanda, NY 14150

www.kidscanpress.com

The artwork in this book was rendered in Photoshop.
The text is set in Animated Gothic.

Edited by Yvette Ghione
Designed by Marie Bartholomew
Printed and bound in Singapore

This book is smyth sewn casebound.

CM 09 0 9 8 7 6 5 4 3 2 1

Library and Archives Canada Cataloguing in Publication
Oldland, Nicholas, 1972–
Big bear hug / written and illustrated by Nicholas Oldland.

ISBN 978-1-55453-464-7

1. Bears—Juvenile fiction. I. Title.

PS8629.L46B54 2009   jC813'.6   C2009-900708-8

Kids Can Press is a **l'O'ру'S**™ Entertainment company

BIG BEAR HUG

Nicholas Oldland

Kids Can Press

There once was a bear so filled with love and happiness that whenever he roamed the forest and came across another living thing, he would give it a hug.

Everywhere he wandered, the bear shared his love hug by hug.

He even hugged creatures that bears have been known to eat. This bear could meet the roundest little rabbit, and he would just stop, smile and give it a great big hug.

No animal was too big ...

Too small ...

Too smelly ...

Or too scary to hug.

But what this bear loved to hug most were the trees.

The bear never met a tree he did not like.

Big trees ...

Little trees ...

Apple trees ...

Pear trees ...

Peach trees.

This bear hugged them all.

One day while the bear was trying to hug a
beaver and a tree at the same time, he noticed
a man with an axe walking into the forest.

The bear followed the man until he stopped at one of the tallest, oldest and most beautiful trees in the forest. The man spent so much time looking at this magnificent tree that the bear thought he must love trees, too.

But to the bear's horror, the man started
to chop the tree down.

For the first time in his life, the bear didn't
feel like hugging at all.

Then, just as he was about to sink his teeth into the man, the bear stopped.

He realized that no matter how angry he was, he simply could not eat the man. It just wasn't in his nature. The bear sighed. And then he decided to do what he did best.

He gave the man a HUG!

The man was not used to getting real big
bear hugs, so once the bear let go, the man
dropped his axe and ran far, far away.

And do you know what the bear did next?

The bear smiled and gave
the tree a great big hug.

The tree felt much better.